Cancer Journal

Written By
Brenda Young Montgomery

CANCER JOURNAL

ISBN 978-1-940831-63-3

Published by Mocy Publishing, LLC.

Website: www.mocypublishing.com

Email: info@mocypublishing.com

Phone: (833) 736-5483

INTRODUCTION

It sneaks in and you think it's your friend. You cuddle it and pamper it to get comfortable. It's calm for a while so you push any thought of anxieties aside. Each day you go on your daily activity not thinking about it but it is still there. It's your body and you don't feel any harm, this is a part of you, a friend. Friends don't bring harm to a friend. We go to sleep together and wake together and there is no fear at all. The friend began to grow and make a stronger presence. The pain and outside appearance started to become a nuisance. My friend started to require more attention and became more and more demanding. It wants more attention since you are supposed to be friends.

After praying and meditating on the matter, my flesh began to interfere with my spiritual soul. It had started to become evident that this friend had been in disguise all alone. What I thought was a friend was an enemy lurking within. I am thankful for my faith and belief that the spirit of the Lord lives and will confirm what is real or counterfeit.

It was wise to seek advice from my physician who confirmed my findings. This began a series of testing that would give the direction in dealing with the enemy dwelling in my body. The enemy will infiltrate in whatever way is beneficial to kill, steal and destroy.

WE CANNOT LET THE ENEMY WIN THIS BATTLE

Self-breast examination has always been a standard procedure. One night in April 2019, I thought the results would be the same. There was a noticeable change, but I tried convincing myself that it was nothing. I shrugged it off for a while as if it was a minor thing and not to worry. After checking each night and feeling uncomfortable the reality of life took over. This could not be anything, my book had just been published and everything was going fine. Sometime different situations we do not plan shows up in our lives. We face them with faith and a positive acceptance. My flesh had almost convinced me to wait for the yearly mammogram which was a month away. After pondering the issue and realizing that it was not my imagination, seeking medical advice was important. We cannot put our health on hold because of fear. We need complete positive energy from beginning to end.

My primary doctor's appointment was already scheduled, so this concern would be discussed. An examination was performed and confirmed that my discovery was real. Before leaving, my mammogram appointment was made to avoid waiting.

The days went by not to think about it, but our human side takes over our thoughts. After yearly mammograms returning negative, regular self-examinations that gave no signs of problems, this was a startling find. In the days ahead the need to not think about what had not been confirmed was important. Sometime our mind will try to put a negative in our thought process and cause confusion and fear.

The mammogram and ultrasound were done. It was confirmed there was something that needed further study. Thinking back over the event, the thought of fear did not

enter in, only to think positive of the journey ahead.
After a biopsy was done, an early-stage cancer was the
prognosis. This was a big surprise and left me speechless
for a moment. This was not something that had ever
crossed my mind in the sickness area.

This discovery required more testing through an MRI.
This test showed a suspicious growth not seen on the
ultrasound. Now another biopsy was scheduled for that
area. It was confirmed the testing showed an early-stage
cancer. Praying and consoling myself to not let pity or
sadness allow me to be sidetracked. Everything was
going great in my life according to what I could see. The
Lord has answered many of my prayers. I will not look
at this as a punishment but as a new direction the Lord
has prepared for me.

After putting everything in prospective, it will be a
new journey not planned. Having faith and keeping a

7

positive attitude from the initial findings, through treatment will be very important in my healing. The recipe for healing is to not concentrate on your sickness but looking forward to your recovery victory.

There were different CT Scans scheduled to make sure no other areas had been infiltrated. After completing all testing, a meeting with the surgeon was scheduled. On May 29, the surgeon gave my husband and I the diagnosis and the surgery choices available for us. We discussed Lumpectomy which would remove a portion of the breast tissue. This surgery would have a higher risk of recurrence of the cancer. Mastectomy surgery would be removing the entire breast, having a greater chance in preventing recurrent breast cancer.

All my 72 years of dealing with different challenges, this was one that never came to mind. Working, healthy and busy with various activities, sickness never brought me down. Now I am faced with a decision, which will affect my body, mind and spirit. While meditating on these developments in my life, I could feel my flesh and spirit having a battle. When you are praying and praising the Lord daily, interference shows up trying to change your thoughts of life, it is a battle. I know my strength and faith is all depending on the guidance from the Lord. I could feel the flesh get weak from fear, but the spirit started whispering (2 Timothy 1:7) "for God hath not given us the spirit of fear; but of power and of love, and of a sound mind."

When I came to myself that this body does not belong to me and it will be changed one day, why should I think that this would affect my life or daily living? Also studying the scripture, (Matt. 5:29-30) tells us it's profitable that one of your members to be cut off from the whole body.

After praying, the decision was made to continue our trust in the Lord, who would bring me through. I questioned the Lord about the 2019 vision board I made early in the year. Reading the list that I wanted to accomplish, cancer was not in the picture. The spirit of the Lord reminded me the board was my vision. The spirit also reminded me that my flesh would not put anything negative in my vision. I began to realize that Cancer would be a strengthening armor that would build my faith stronger than ever. My main ingredient was to be strong and of good courage, knowing the battle was not mine, but the Lord. When looking back on years of conquering various difficulties and overcoming them, even when not the results I wanted, my spirit shouted with joy. Sometimes, we receive journeys that will test our faith and belief, to confirm who we really are in the walk of Christianity. I have had years of struggles that tried to pull me off the road of straight. We try not to give in to this society we live. When we least expected, something shows up in our lives that requires special attention. This is how I am taking hold of my life issues that is at hand with prayer and faith.

My surgeon scheduled the surgery for Wednesday, July 10. The family was informed of the surgery date. My husband has been by my side through each ordeal. Our support for each other in whatever task we had to endure, always gave the strength to make it.

Even though we told the family out of town all was well, since I had support of my husband along with my brother and family, that did not matter or prevent them from showing up. Our daughter, son, grandson and sisters showed up to give support. It was a great joy to spend time with them before the surgery. Teaching Sunday school with them present was special. The spirit guided me in teaching the lesson, without my display of what I would be facing in the coming days. I am thankful for the strength that my faith and belief have given me.

The family was busy taking the burden off my husband. They were busy keeping the house in order with whatever the need. There was the aroma of soul food constantly filling the house atmosphere. This was a fellowship with love and care shown to each other. This display was such a spirit lifter to delete any negative spirit that would try to get in.

The days before surgery were filled with laughter and compassion. We did not miss a day of remembering the days of our youth and the times spent with our parents. It was special learning about the tricks we all played on each other. All of these conversations were a great therapy for each of us to make it through the journey.

The Lord put who He wanted in each family for a reason. We each have our strengths and weaknesses, but together we stand and divided we fall. Prayers, faith and love we shared for Jesus, would keep us strong during this journey.

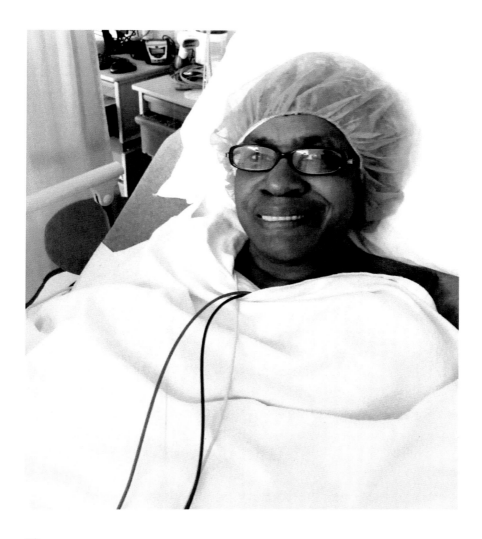

The morning of surgery is here, and I am ready spiritually. The paperwork procedure was complete for admittance. The waiting room is filled with family, friends and church family. Now in the preparation room, nurses are busy setting up the steps needed before going into the surgical area. I am observing the team as they prepare me for surgery, not worried, but as if no emotion at all. There was no memory from the time going into the operating room, told to breathe into the mask, next thing awakening in the recovery room. It was a feeling of peace that took me far away. I had put my trust in the Lord that this was the journey chosen for me to be a testimony for someone else.

The nurses were so amazed at my alertness after the surgery. It was such a joy in the recovery room seeing my family and the relief on their faces showing that they were relieved that the surgery was a success. I know it was a stressful time for all of them in the not knowing. When someone is having surgery of any kind, the feeling of uncertainty comes over you. It is only when we let our faith kick in and take over our mind is when we find safety.

I felt as if nothing had taken place, except looking at the bandage wrappings which also had two small bottles connecting tubing for drainage. I called them my buddies, because they would be with me for a while. It was such a blessing to have no pains. All vitals were good and no evidence of infection. Usually after anesthesia the patient is left with drowsiness or still sleeping. I was alert and in good spirit. While getting situated in my room for the night, the family was arranging who would be staying. I tried explaining that no one was needed to be with me. My husband was overruled by our daughter, who thought he needed to go home and get some rest with the family. Evidently my input did not matter because our daughter ended up staying, watching me like a hawk. The good news was that I was able to have soft intake and drink some juice that night.

The next day I was feeling great and able to eat breakfast. Now that the surgery was complete, there was such a relief knowing the threat to my body had been solved. Although I knew this was only the beginning of the healing process. The surgeon visited me that morning and gave me more confidence that surgery went well and mentioned I was such a great patient. She stated my vitals were registering normal, my discharge would be scheduled. Since the discharge papers would take a while, lunch was ordered. After finishing my lunch, preparation was being made for my departure.

Instructions were discussed with the discharge nurse of steps pertaining to the drainage tube. The whole ordeal had not registered in my mind of what was to follow. The Lord prepares us for all assignments given from the beginning to ending with faith and courage.

Arriving home was such a feeling of joy and happiness. The house smelled of great home cooking, which was a relief after hospital food. I did not waste any time feasting on each dish. We began talking about the family waiting to be called in the recovery room. They all stated of being nervous during the surgery hours. The unknown will always put us in a state of concern. I expressed how fortunate it was to have family there through this challenge. We all need family and friend support while we are going through any situation.

It seemed as though nothing had changed, but it had. As I began to get freshened for the night's rest it really began to hit me. After taking off the bra that was placed during surgery, my emotions began to react. I knew that a part of me was taken but until I saw the spot where it was, tears began to shed. I know that the breast had to leave because of the tumor but to see it gone was so hurting. It was an emotional time for me that night. I did not want my family to see me and get worried. We all experience times of weakness that tries to enter our minds. Even though we pray and have faith it happens. After getting a grip on myself, I started to remember the scripture that tells us to lose a member and save the body. I began to give thanks and praises to the Lord for bringing me through. My faith kept me from feeling sorry for myself, to stay strong and be a witness for someone else along the way.

My family was amazed at my recovery and the attitude I had in preparing myself for the next step.

Having faith in the Lord gives strength and confidence in any situation we are faced. I arrived home where the display of love continued. There were outpouring of flowers and cards from family and friends. The neighbors offered assistance in my convalescing care. Their visits and get-well wishes were appreciated.

The family is preparing to return to their various locations.   We hated to see them leave but knew their visit was temporary. The house had been filled with the aroma of different recipes.   They really had the food menu together and each dish was good. It felt great to be waited on but I would forget sometime because of my independence. Not having to cook or clean was great and I almost got use to.   It is always such a great joy to have a family that is concerned about your wellbeing. Treating each other with respect and a caring spirit is the love that the Lord tells us about.

The weekly visit from the nurse, physical therapist and occupational therapist were being scheduled. The nurse came to check the tubing discharge and gave such special care. There was a daily journal kept marking the drainage count from the tubing each day.

My niece came to assist emptying the drainage tubes on days the nurse did not come. She was available to assist my husband with caring for my needs. We really appreciated her care and concern which was such a great help during my convalescing. The reports from the nurse were good and not much drainage on the pads. Everything was going great with the drainage and I was not having any pain. Each day showed less drainage, which was great news because that would determine how soon the tubing would be taken out.

The tubing led drainage into two small bottles. The bottles hung down and would make me uncomfortable.

Not laying on that side became normal because it prevented anything that would handicap my healing process. It took much strength and will not to go back in the past before finding the tumor. Having a strong faith foundation was the only reason I was able to hold myself together. It is not easy to stay focused on the journey when the enemy tries to invade your thoughts.

July 23, 2019 was my visit with the surgeon. My spirit was high since my visit with her before surgery. I have accepted the journey with faith and keeping a very positive attitude.

She stated everything was looking great. The tubes began showing smaller amount of drainage. It was a relief when I heard the tubing would be taken out. It took a while to get used to those bottles hanging down. I started calling them my buddies, because they were with me all the time. Such a relief now to lay on my side again, although at times I would forget that they were not there any longer.

Today is quiet with sunshine beaming through the window. Since the family left my husband has been taking great care of me. I tell everyone that he still has me on lock down. When you are used to doing everything, it is hard to change. This is the time for me to be obedient and let the healing take place. Convalescing gives you a since of peace that cannot be described. On July 30, 2019 my visit to my surgeon was inspiring. After checking my surgical area she was amazed how it was healing, she stated that it looked beautiful. The stitching was arranged so neatly. I had to control my composure seeing the area where the breast once was. I recalled the conversation with the surgeon before surgery. She mentioned the choice of implants while the surgery would be taking place. Before I could respond my husband stated that I did not need any implants. Jokingly I stated, suppose I want to get an upgrade. This brought a burst of laughter in the room. Of course the decision was decided against putting me through any additional trauma that would only be for outer appearance.

After putting everything in prospective, it will be a journey not planned but achieved. Having faith and keeping a positive attitude from the initial findings, through the treatment designed for me, will be very important in my healing. The recipe for healing is to not concentrate on your sickness but looking forward to your recovery victory.

My surgery is completed but it was only the beginning of what lied ahead. Listening to my doctors and nurses, being obedient to the therapist, maintaining a healthy diet will give me strength to prepare for the treatment decided.

The physical and occupational therapist met with me to schedule my regimens. I am still being positive in this journey, taking each day as the road to my healing. Doing the different exercises have not been difficult. I am so grateful for the strength that the Lord has given me. There are moments that my emotions try to sneak upon me but staying focused on the finished line brings me back to reality. The words of my caregivers, family and friends gave me the motivation to keep striving for the goal that was reachable.

The Lord sent a nurse that was a breast cancer survivor to care for me. Her spirit was remarkable. She kept telling me of my positive spirit. I informed her that she showed me that this was not an ending event. I know that the Lord had sent her to me to be a witness that

He is no respect of person. After thanking the Lord for sending me such great people, little did I know he would send a therapist who had recovered from a double mastectomy. All of these remarkable people are still busy in their careers being an inspiration to others.

July 31, 2019 I am scheduled for a throat biopsy. This was related to the CT scan given before my surgery. While in the procedure room waiting for the testing, I began staring at the light in the ceiling. It was as though I was put in a trance from what was going on in the room. My prayers asked for strength to overpower fear while the testing was being done. The doctors and nurses were very caring and polite. The procedure was complete, now to wait on the diagnosis. I will not let thoughts of fear interfere with the healing that is already taking place.

The physical therapist directed me to the steps to strengthen my lower body functions. I was able to perform various exercises with no problem. Each visit my vitals were all good. It was stated that because of my being active before the surgery was helping. Their main emphasis was to build my strength for when the treatments began. I would be energetic for each visit knowing that I had to stay focused on the end results. I have been gradually doing light duty to keep my limbs functioning. Keeping in mind I am still not back to my standard activity level. It is amazing when you look back over your life and daily mind set, it is only when you find out for yourself that each day bring about a new challenge. The therapist gave encouragement on how eager I was to attempt all assignments. He told me that I was an exceptional patient and did not need any more visits.

The occupational therapist directed me to strengthen my upper body. She complimented how great and strong I was becoming. She explained that visiting many patients within the week, my attitude and motivation was amazing. It was expressed that to have such great vitals from the surgery and each therapy visit, words could not describe. I explained that I am nothing without the spirit of the Lord.

I do not feel uneasy when making that statement. Sometimes we find ourselves shying away from letting people know about our spiritual side. I am so excited to tell anyone and everyone how good the Lord has been to me. It was always a joy when she would come for my therapy treatments. It seemed as if this was a friend coming to visit. The therapist visit went well. Conquering the different exercise regimens are beginning to make me feel stronger and my mind is at ease.

Although not knowing what lies ahead for me, it is as if in a daze, taking steps as though being led. The last day of therapy was a downer for us but a blessing that the Lord put us together.

August 5, 2019, I visited the oncologist to get the results of the throat biopsy. Praise the Lord it was benign. The doctor gave me encouragement while I continue waiting for the pathologist report. She stated that it was a small percentage chemo may be needed. I told her my prayer is whatever the Lord's will for me. I am not waking each day worrying about what lies ahead for me, only giving praise each new day. There are some emotional days that try to take over my thoughts. Those are the times that I think back over my life, where the Lord has brought me. The inward grounding of the Word that is instilled in you gives joy and strength to snap out of that state of mind. Being in a world where so much is going on, even though it doesn't involve you, there is a distraction that causes a bit of sadness.

While going through the struggles of life in the midst of the cancer discovery, depression almost had a hold on me. I was nearly blinded of plans for the future. One day as if in a dream and awakened, I knew that my guardian angel was leading me and not letting my decision become flawed. My body is still in the healing process even though my strength is good. August 9, 2019, I received a call from the radiologist office that my appointment for Monday needed to be cancelled since my pathologist report had not been returned. First, I was beginning to get upset and disgusted. That was the instinct of my flesh rebelling to the situation. Waiting on anything can be done with patience or anxiety. My flesh wanted to hurry the results to get to the solution. Not until I realized that the solution the Lord had for me was not going to change and my patience and endurance had to take heed.

On August 12, 2019 I wanted to attend church but my husband reminded me quoting a great man that we knew, "don't make your move to soon". He reminded me that my faithfulness would not be tarnished because of not visiting the worship place. He stated my spirit was still worshiping by praying, reading my Sunday school lessons and studying the Word. We know that attending a worship place is important, being among other believers. But it is only the Lord that knows your true sense of relationship with Him. He stated that my body still needed me to focus on total healing which comes by faith and rest. We all need to have someone in their life to keep our focus on the end results.

On August 19, 2019 is a visit with the oncologist. My vitals were good and news that I would not need to have chemo was a great blessing. When hearing that news, there was a burst of thank you Jesus, tears of joy with hugs and smiles. It wasn't that I knew what would be involved with chemo treatment other than being a more detailed treatment to the body.

On August 20, 2019 was a visit to the radiologist. Vitals are taken and all is good. The doctor came into the room with a pleasant smile. He began to tell us of the decision of radiation treatment had been decided. It was stated this would be a precautionary treatment given to the wall where the tumors were taken. This treatment would kill any micro cell tissues that would have been able to grow and become a problem later. He stated that normally 16-20 treatments are prescribed but would be adjusted if needed. My spirit was calm and accepted the plan as described. The preliminary setup was done to prepare the area for treatment. Now waiting for the call giving the date treatments are to begin. I am feeling great and looking forward to completing this chapter and move on to what is to follow.

Sunday, August 25, 2019 was my first Sunday back to church since July 7, 2019. It was a great feeling to receive communion. Everyone greeted me with such warm and compassion spirits. I do not take anything for granted. My outer display is to show someone else that the Lord is no respect of person. What strength and faith he gives to me is available for anyone who lets Him in. The church members mentioned that my appearance did not show any display of sickness. I remember the teachings that we had received from our Pastor, that if we have faith our outer body should not show what we are going through. It was such a great celebration in showing how great the Lord is to those that put their trust in Him. If you have joy in the inside it will shine on the outside.

August 27, 2019 is a follow up with my primary doctor. She was very excited of how I was healing and with such spunk. My vitals were great so I was told to continue doing the steps necessary for healing. After leaving and returning home my spirit was great. We noticed a missed call from the radiologist. Happy this would be the call for beginning treatment. After calling them back, I found out they wanted me to return for another marking measurement. On Wednesday, August 28, 2019 I went to the appointment. They explained due to organs located on my left side, they wanted different angles to proceed with my treatment. Mainly, they wanted to have the best position for my safety. It was beginning to be upsetting, waiting and waiting to begin the treatments. Until I got a grip on myself and stopped the anxiety in it tracks, my mood began to keep a positive outlook.

That special call came giving me the date of my first treatment. Would you believe they have it scheduled on my birthday, September 4, 2019? They mentioned changing it to another day but I wanted to get started on the journey ahead.

Sunday, September 1, 2019 I went to church, giving praise for my healing and such strength during my road of recovery. It was a sense of joy and gratefulness to the Lord for all He had done to able me to walk and drive. Being greeted with smiles and caring spirits from the worshippers was very uplifting. The most important thing is showing that the Lord is no respect of person. When we become afflicted, it is nothing that we have done to cause it. It is not a curse put on us by the Lord.

If we acknowledge it as a test of our faith and trust in believing that the Lord will bring us through completely. There is always someone being used as a testimony to confirm the workings of the Lord and give Him praise.

Monday, September 2, 2019, was a celebrating holiday for most. Twenty-three years ago today my mother left to be with the Lord. I began remembering the good parenting provided and the love she always displayed. Such great sadness that she is not here to give me comfort during this ordeal. It was a day that year of great loss when knowing I would not hear her voice again in my ear. The memories reflect how important it is to always show love each day. We never know what the next day will bring and change your life. I am so thankful that she showed me what love and caring is all about. Especially grateful that she knew the Lord and taught us all about Him.

It was strange when touching my left breast and not having any feeling. The touch was as a shallow with no interior. I am looking forward as the days goes by to see the transforming and the sensitivity. There are tears of joy flowing because of being thankful for a successful operation. I may have lost a member of my body but have increased in faith and love. Each new day I can feel the sensation returning to that area.

1st Radiation Treatment – September 4, 2019

I woke this morning feeling great and in good spirit on my birthday.   The day began giving praise for the blessings that the Lord has provided. Thankful the Lord kept the hedge of protection and gave me life to a brand-new day. I am ready for my treatment with a positive attitude not knowing what is involved.   Entering the cancer center, being greeted with a smile and caring spirit from everyone.   Entering the changing room are other patients waiting for their treatment. Some showed the composure of uncertainty and nervousness. I began to minister a word of encouragement that we all needed to hear. I reminded everyone that the center was the place to be energized from our sickness. We have to motivate each other and not leave from the treatment the same way we showed up.

After lying on the bed in the treatment room, the techs gave instructions to line up the markings with the machine. It was a weird feeling seeing this machine traveling over me with a red line, which was probably the release of radiation. The room gave me a sense of calmness and secure feeling. Looking at the ceiling display was so refreshing. My body began to relax to the atmosphere. The treatment lasted about 10 minutes. After completion I felt fine and with no loss of energy. They really made my day before I left the location. I was presented with a birthday gift bag. There are such great caring people still around. It is always a blessing to have people that think not only of themselves but others.

After leaving my treatment it was a day of celebrating a new day that the Lord had allowed me. I celebrated my birthday with a great meal prepared by my husband. We talked about the strength and faith I had displayed to the fellow patients that were seen. My husband witnessed the warmth and compassion that each patient received from the center's workers. My day would end with preparation for my next visit to the treatment center.

Celebrating another treatment day.

2nd Radiation Treatment – September 5, 2019

Today is a day of gladness and fresh grace. After a
night of restlessness and concern of the journey ahead, I
felt a relief of joy breaking through. We have to prepare
our mind for all the negative forces that try to enter in. I
have made a decision not to be defeated by the devices of
the enemy.   After arriving to the center and directed to
the changing area, there were a few patients waiting. We
began talking with each other regarding our various
ailments. Until you listen to someone else talk about
what they are dealing with, it sinks in that you are not
alone. I thank the Lord for not having the spirit of fear.
Listening to what some are dealing with and the concern
they all had was unreal. My spiritual man took control of
the room. My faith and caring spirit radiated unto the
room. They all knew the Lord but still needed

motivation and encouragement. We all become weak at times, so the Lord places us in the right places at the right time. We each went to our treatment room knowing that our strength had been revived. A kind word gives the courage and motivation needed to make it. In the treatment room is a quietness which sends such a comforting spirit. It is as if you are not in control of anything for a few moments. My treatment went well and I look forward to the journey ahead. The doctor had previously checked the area being treated and explained the area was looking well.

Once leaving the treatment center there was a great feeling of strength. After seeing the other patients arriving to get what they each needed to restore their health, it was evident that I'm not in this battle alone. Each sickness that we incur has to be dealt with faith, courage and strength to hold a positive attitude. After leaving the center I am full of faith and continue to show that this is a temporary season of a new test of faith.

Celebrating another treatment day

3rd Radiation Treatment – September 6, 2019

Today, to awake in the right mind set is a blessing. It is known what happened yesterday but today is an unknown. Praying and giving thanks for health and strength is important. Even though yesterday's testing went well, the body is going through challenges not experienced before. Staying positive and believing the journey is only temporary. After arriving and preparing for the treatment, there was a since of calmness and anxiousness of what was to happen. Even though it is the same treatment, no one knows the end results. Having faith and trust has brought me thus far and will take me to the finish line. The calmness in the treatment room was amazing. Looking at the ceiling always gave a sense of security or protection. The appearance reflects a scenery that puts you in a relaxed state. It is such a special blessing of restoring strength. The treatment went well, and I am always reminded to leave with encouraging words to those waiting. Since we would not have treatment on the weekends everyone was excited.

Some patients were happy to have some days off because of the type of treatment they received. I reminded them that even though treatment may cause pain, the end result is the healing they will receive. I know firsthand about pain and suffering. Therefore, I am focused on each instruction given to me that will lead to my healing.

I am continuing my day with a positive attitude and praise for the strength given to me to be a light to someone else.

Celebrating another treatment day

4th Radiation Treatment – September 9, 2019

This morning I woke with thanksgiving in my heart, grateful for this new day and excited that this is a day of treatment. The rain during the night left dampness and coolness. The weather has its way of sometime putting you in a different frame of mind. Even the squirrels did not show any energy shaking acorns from the tree. If we are not careful, the weather can put you in a mood of sadness or depression. Always appreciate whatever forecast each day brings and embrace it with joy. After placing the thoughts in its perspectives, I began to embrace getting ready for going to the treatment. After arriving, I was directed to the changing room area. After your first visit you know the procedure. Entering the area there were patients waiting. I changed and joined them, since we had not seen each other for two days. We began to all talk about our journey. Each day meeting different patients, all dealing with various circumstances but having similar ailments. I began to realize that diseases do not discriminate. We are different ethnicity, but we hurt, feel pain, fear the unknown and want to be healed. Cancer brings all of us together, it doesn't matter who you are or what you have. It attacks the body and cling to any area.

The treatment team becomes familiar with the patients. The team shows care and compassion. It is comforting for a patient to be treated with kindness. In the room the machine does the job which last 10 minutes. Being left in a room with machines traveling over you, with red lines in some area and making noises, would make you uncomfortable. After asking questions of how everything worked my confidence became strong. The treatment techs knew their jobs and did them with such professionalism.

Arriving home and I began to work in the yard. The flowers always give you a perk watching how they seem to grow. Even though they are blooming, weeds seem to always try to sneak in. It makes you think about how the enemy attacks our bodies the same way. We make sure to free the flowers and plants from weeds. It is our responsibility to do the same for our bodies when it is under attack.

Celebrating another treatment day

5th Radiation Treatment – September 10, 2019

Such a lovely day, sunshine makes you think summer is just beginning. It is such a blessing to be feeling strong and full of energy. The treatment has it purpose to eliminate the invaders in our bodies. As we all started arriving to the center, greeting each other with love and concern about our individual treatments. Some patients receiving chemo and radiation need a higher level of energy. Knowing what they have to endure, I do not complain about my journey. Each new day is a blessing. In the treatment room is the delight of calmness and comfort. The spirit provides the positive feeling that everything will be alright. After each treatment my body is receiving the energy to combat this enemy name cancer. It fights to take over but strength and will power will not let it succeed. Each day after treatment I feel as if the body is building a energized wall that will combat any intruding disease.

After cleansing each morning and night, there is a healing cream applied to the area that is being treated. Remember the radiation is energy to kill any disease cell that is trying to live. The area has to be treated with care so that it will receive a minimal amount of irritation.

Celebrating another day of treatment

6th Radiation Treatment – September 11, 2019

The weather report is predicting storms but it still displays the look of a summer day. No matter the weather, my treatment is still on schedule. It is an appointment that you do not want to change or miss. The temperature today is hot but still a blessing to see. I arrived at the center and started my usual routine. Once in the changing room it's a different atmosphere. We are all there for various treatments. We greet each other with sincere concern and a very caring spirit. We all have had our pity party at times which did not last long. When you put your trust and faith in our Lord and Savior, we have already overcome. The treatment techs make sure each patient is comfortable and always shows an interest in our state of mind. Today in the treatment room, a negative spirit tried to set in my thoughts. It was only when I looked at the ceiling tile that displayed the blue sky, calmness and peace took over. The enemy is always on attack, but we have to not give in to the trap. After finishing treatment, entering the changing area where the other patients were waiting full of joy and happiness. It gave those waiting a positive feeling beyond what they have to experience.

Celebrating another day of treatment

7th Radiation Treatment – September 12, 2019

This is a new day to give praise for the strength and motivation given during this journey. No matter what it seems in our mind, the way have already been cleared for our healing journey. We do not get to pick how our road of life will be or how it will end. We do have the choice to be determined not to be defeated while traveling this road. Entering the center smiling and greeting the workers and patients was a formality for me. We don't know how each of these individuals day started. The nurse took my vitals and they were good. The doctor checked my treated area and stated it looked great. It was mentioned that the skin was not showing any sign of irritation. Using the cream that was recommended was doing the job.

The treatment techs were waiting with their compassion and caring spirit, as they carried out the treatment. While in the treatment room there is a calm feeling. The ceiling had such a great display of colors. It seemed as if being in a garden on flowers. The tiles had changed into pictures of a blue sky with clouds all around. I felt as if this was a place of safety and not fear. Treatment is complete and I feel as if part of me was left in the room. When entering the changing room, the patients waiting said I had a very refreshed appearance. I stated that my faith removed any fear that tried to enter. Each treatment day I am left with such gratefulness to the doctors, nurses and all the techs.

Celebrating another day of treatment

8th Radiation Treatment – September 13, 2019

Today is a blessing to know that I am halfway to the end of treatment. I woke with a smile giving thanks for this new day. After having such a restful night with no pain was a great feeling of refreshment. We take for granted when lying down that we will see a new day. It is only a gift of new breath that the Lord breathed into our nostril, because our work on earth is still needed.

Entered into the waiting area and prepared for the treatment. The techs were ready, energetic as usual. The machines did their scanning of the area while I watched their every move. I could not help but think how science had improved in procedures to cure various diseases. The machines traveling over you and treating the areas marked were remarkable. Those are thoughts that I had while in this treating room alone. The scenery in the tiles, seem so bright and real. It puts your mind in a peaceful state that relaxes the body. I am thankful that my faith is strong and will not waiver.

The treatment is complete for today. It was a joy greeting patients while returning to the changing room with the spirit of hope. It was so important for my outer person to show a display of strength and motivation to those waiting to be treated.

Everyone excited today that it is Friday and no treatments on the weekend. We all gave our exiting words of safety and looking forward to seeing each other on Monday. This was not considered a doctor visit to me when attending my treatments. I have accepted this assignment and will travel the journey with faith, hope and strength to the end.

After getting home we started working in the yard. It gives such joy pampering the flowers and the vegetables. There is no better therapy than to see the change in what you have planted. It is a display seeing that you planted and the Lord is in charge of the growth.

Celebrating another day of treatment

NO TREATMENT – September 14, 2019

I woke feeling great with a lot of energy. Started doing the laundry, making trips up and down the stairs helped build my leg strength. As to not push myself into fatigue, remembering the words of my therapist, I took breaks in between my walks. The garden is blooming with vegetables and the flowers are standing tall displaying such beautiful colors. The squirrels are enjoying jumping from limb to limb. On some occasions they chase each other up the tree. It is so fascinating how they swing on the tree limbs. I started looking at the black squirrels and trying to figure out when that color showed up. It tells us we do not have any control of creation. It is very important to stay focused on my healing and not get sidetracked. Our mind pushes us because of our past activities. The body can only heal while we are resting. I am praying that my body will be

strong enough to attend church this Sunday.

NO TREATMENT – September 15, 2019

My day started with thanks in my heart and praise on my lips. Last night the fatigue feeling tried to find a spot in my mind. Sometimes we start thinking about what we are dealing with and the enemy sneaks in. This trap was caught and destroyed before getting in. When awakening this morning I was feeling great and full of vigor to attend church. The spirit of the Lord will keep us safe and secure if we believe in him.

Sunday school was a great appetizer preparing for our morning sermon learning about Jesus. Your spiritual life will not grow until we know who Jesus is. I know that my strength has grown because of faith and belief that I will be healed. Church members were excited to see how the Lord was blessing me. It was stated that my outer appearance did not show sickness. I was excited to get a refuel of spiritual energy for my week ahead. We have to always pray and give thanks for each new day with courage and positive spirit.

9th Radiation Treatment – September 16, 2019

This is a new day of grace and mercy given to me. I am watching the tree limbs move and the squirrels chasing each other's. You can see them running up the trees, knocking the acorns down as they swing from limb to limb. They can be seen eating some acorns and burying for the winter. Oh how marvelous is the creation.

Once entering the cancer building, I could feel a burst of joy and happiness. This may seem strange to some to say that but everything we encounter builds our faith. We can all look back over our lives and see the pain and struggles we have survived.   Everything we encounter will be a lesson in some way or another.

Being greeted by staff with great words of kindness make you feel so special. Patients in the changing room were full of smiles. There was a feeling of happiness, even though treatment had not received been as of yet. Now in the treatment room the techs guide me into the position needed for the machine to detect the area for treatment. Once positioning they leave the room and treatment begins. The machine glides over my body, a red light shining above. Being still but my eyes are taking notice watching the red lines on the machine as it travels. The ceiling tiles are bursting with colors and fern plants that seem to be moving by a wind. I know they are not real but it put a sense of calmness in the room. It is amazing how much advance technology to cure a disease there is. Treatment is complete, I am feeling great. I gave my thanks and appreciation to all of their caring spirit.

Celebrating another day of treatment

10th Radiation Treatment – September 17, 2019

Another day the Lord has blessed me to see. Last night was filled with sadness for a moment but laughter and joy seemed to take over. When thinking about the blessings I have received, peace gave me comfort. Remembering months ago of love ones, ending their battle with various diseases, my mind began to be overwhelmed. We have to put each day in its perspectives because we never know what lies ahead for us. Arriving at the cancer center today I was full of joy and greeted them with a smile showing an uplifting spirit. Unless you are going through or have been in these situations you don't know what it's like.

Entering into the treatment room, I am ready to be obedient to the tech's instructions. Our main objective is to be healed. Unless we accept and follow the guidelines given for our recovery, we come in vain. I am determined to follow every instruction given to me. In the treatment room the techs aligned my body according to the markings. The machine is moving to perform its duty. While staring into the ceiling when the machine passes over, along with the tiny red light was something unique. As I looked up there it was, that caught my attention. I had glanced at it before but until today it had a different meaning. The pictures of flowers, bright and colorful reminded me of the plants and flowers I care for at home. Their display was offering such a display of calmness, showing no weeds trying to infiltrate. I am so excited that the Lord is keeping me in perfect peace.

The treatment ended well with prayer that the mission was being accomplished. I left the center giving encouragement and motivation to the patients waiting for treatment.

Celebrating another day of treatment

11th Radiation Treatment – September 18, 2019

Sun shining bright today and the temperature is beginning to get warm. No matter the weather it would not change my mood. Staying completely focused on my healing regimens was my main concern. Last night the negative spirit tried to enter in my mind but I was able to not let anything change my positive state of mind. My husband seems to give encouraging words when needed. When we start to get in a different state of mind, we need someone to help bring out the negative trance that may be trying to get in.

The cancer center was already active with patients arriving in changing room.   We always talk about the various incidents that led to where we are. We gave thanks to each other for the caring words of kindness. Put in mind of gathering at church with thanks and praise in our heart. The church, a hospital also for the sick knowing everything is in the Lord's hand. The Cancer Center also the hospital with the knowledge needed to assist in our healing process but also guided by the Lord.

Now in the treatment room being instructed and positioned by the techs. As the machine travels over me I could see the ceiling with the tiny red light still there. Some of the tiles are pictures of blue sky with a display of clouds within. I started praising the Lord for his creation. The view gave me a sense of peace as a reminder of God's presence even in the treatment room. Even with everything going on, I know who is in control. This room has become a place of prayer and thanksgiving. Treatment is complete, and the techs stated that everything went well and see you tomorrow. I gave my thanks for their kindness and promptness.

Celebrating another day of treatment

12th Radiation Treatment – September 19, 2019

Good morning to a sunny but nice cool day. The birds were singing a soothing melody, the squirrels chasing each other jumping from limb to limb. Seeing how the animals show no sign of fear, confirm that as the Lord provide for them, He is always watching over me. Now it's time to begin the trip for my treatment. I am still excited and motivated to complete this journey. I greeted the patients and workers as I entered the building. The techs always had such a caring spirit. That means a lot to a patient when someone shows kindness and concern to them. No one knows what each of us has to endure in order to make it to the treatments. There are those who depend on transportation service or relative and friends to get them to the center. I am thankful for having a concerned family and husband that goes on every treatment or doctor appointments.

Now the techs are getting me in position on the table. The machine starts moving, giving the treatment of today. As it moved, I stared at the ceiling that displayed a fern plant within the tile. I pretended that the wind was moving each leaf. The clouds are giving a display as if being a security cover. The blue sky in the background is such a delight. The treatment time is already up, which seemed so short. It was only because of the peace that this room brings.

Celebrating another day of treatment

13th Radiation Treatment – September 20, 2019

Today brought a bright ray of sunshine and great weather. You would think summer is just beginning. I soon woke up to the reality that fall was lurking. I am feeling great joy and a refreshing spirit. My mind is always giving thanks and praise for my healing each day. Cancer does not discriminate. It attacks anyone and any part of the body. Do not think if you are young or old it can't show up. I have gotten past the shock and wondering of what lies ahead. I take each day as a new challenge and purpose. We all have a purpose in life. Not until we accept and take responsibility, the end result will seem unreachable. This is how I have accepted the journey of breast cancer, staying focused on the end result, which is healing.

I entered the building full of motivation and a triumph feeling. Everyone has a smile as we greet each other. I started to prepare for treatment in the waiting area. One of the patients entered after returning from her treatment. She was looking very sad and stated the treatment gear she had to wear was painful. I stated that she continue praying, staying strong and to not focus on the equipment needed to assist in her treatment. We should think only on the end results, which is the healing benefit from the treatments received. We each need someone to give encouragement and support. Encouraging someone else helps to keep me strong.

The techs are ready to position me on the treatment table. I lay as the machine starts the procedure. Each day the treatment seems to be shorter. The room gives such a comfort and secure feeling. Maybe it is because of being relaxed and familiar with what is being done. Treatment is complete for today so we give our cordial greetings, to enjoy the weekend and stay safe.

Celebrating another day of treatment.

NO TREATMENT – September 21, 2019

Today I found myself sleeping late which brought a reminder I heard from the doctor/nurses. They had mentioned that during your last days of treatment you may experience fatigue. I had awaken early but failed to get up and fell back to sleep. It is good because your body heals while resting. Once up I felt refreshed and was ready for my day of activity. It is a joy spending time in the garden and working with the flowers. Seeing the display of various flower colors and the green leaves on the trees was refreshing. It is such a joy how my body is healing. I gave thanks and gratitude to the Lord for where my healing has come. Your mind plays an important part in your healing process. We have to continue being motivated no matter what each day may bring.

NO TREATMENT – September 22, 2019

I woke early this morning giving praise and thanks for this new day. Last night the area being treated tried to stir up pain but I did not let it enter into my mind. The birds are chirping and the squirrels are chasing each others. I felt great after a good night rest which helped with the fatigue. My energy remained high while preparing for Sunday school.

I arrived at church and was received with smiles and caring greetings from the church family. It was such a great feeling to hear the encouraging words of support. Everything was inspiring today which kept me in such a great spirit.

Sunday school always gives such touching reminders within the lesson that is inspiring. It always prepares you for the sermon with an eagerness of what you will hear next. The sermon reminded us our faith should not be at the same level from when we started. It also reminded me my facial expression should display a positive view of the healing power of the Lord.

14th Radiation Treatment – September 23, 2019

I woke early this morning thinking about how the Lord has blessed me. During these last days at times I feel as if fatigue is trying to set in. The cream used on the treated area makes a big difference in the healing process.   Recalling what I had heard during my treatment days is now coming to a reality.   Sleeping later than usual which give the body rest and healing.   I arrived at the center with the usual uplifted spirit.   The workers always greeted me with such courteous and pleasant smiles. As I entered the waiting room a patient entered and was not in the best spirit. She was emotionally drained from the treatments she receives. We greeted each other but she began to tell how tired she was going through the various treatments. I explained that she had to be strong and not concentrate on what she is dealing with. I told her to look back from where she started and that should build up her motivation. We each have to stay encouraged and motivated to build our self-confidence. She stated her desire is to go to sleep and not wake up. My heart became heavy that someone would get into that state of mind. The main thing I mentioned was that each day she wakes up the Lord has work for her to do. I reminded her that each new day awaken gives another treatment to get closer to the final results of her healing goal. It was a pleasure to let her know that encouraging her builds up my confidence. As the techs entered to get her, she thanked me, reached down, and gave me a hug.

It is evident why the Lord is using me as a vessel. It has been a journey that changes with each new day. While in the waiting room, new patients entered and we talk about each of our journeys. Now entering the treatment room, being positioned on the table, my treatment began. The machines move to the areas needing treatment, I stared into the ceiling and gave thanks to the Lord for my healing and the strength to not waiver. Treatment finished and I returned into the waiting room feeling energized.

A patient, waiting for treatment, mentioned having a family history of breast cancer. We talked about having faith in the Lord and doing what it takes for our healing. The tech came for her as I was leaving. We hugged and gave encouragement to each other. This has been a day of tears and smiles.

Celebrating another day of treatment

15th Radiation Treatment – September 24, 2019

Good morning to a new day of grace and mercy. It was such a joy, even though I am going through this journey, it is not viewed as a burden. We have to take each day as a gift that will take us to a destination for our good. While entering the center my attitude is still uplifted. This is the gathering place where we receive a portion of healing treatment. We greet each other with a smile and concern for each other. At this place we see no difference in each other origin. We each have our mind centered on our healing procedures.

We show up and wait patiently for the treatment which will give us a chance of being cured. Staying focused mean a lot in the healing process. The patients were present and in better spirit.   We still gave encouragement and inspired them to stay strong. We met a new patient today during our scheduled time. She stated that this was her first day. I told her to stay strong and encouraged.   It is important not to concentrate on the sickness or the reason for the treatment. We have to keep our mind positive while going through these treatments. It has to be a daily activity.

I am in the treatment room being positioned on the table.   I began to watch as the machines glide over me reminding me of robotics the way they are shaped. They are square and round with different connections moving from one direction to the other.   In these last days of treatment it has been comfortable and warm in this room.   It probably sounds unbelievable but a true statement.   Once treatment completed, the techs stated that everything went well and I did such a great job. I thanked them as usual for their courtesy and greeted the workers and patients as I left.

Celebrating another day of treatment

16th Radiation Treatment - September 25, 2019

(FINAL TREATMENT)

I woke this morning feeling refreshed as usual. It was great looking forward to this new day and all of the blessings. You would think I should be happy to finish my last treatment. For some reason I was beginning to feel a sadness. It was such a blessing lifting the patients spirit that were feeling depressed and energy stressed. The Lord had been so good to me during this time. He has kept me strong and spiritually filled. It has been a journey that was unforeseen but the Lord has given me strength to offer motivation and support. Entering into the center I displayed the same greeting and smile. Even though this would be my last day, I still remained cheerful and energetic.

In the treatment room the techs greeted me with smiles as usual. Now after positioning me on the table aligning with the marked area, the treatment began. The machines started moving about, pinpointing the areas that needed attention. Staring into the ceiling tile with the display of clouds with blue sky background held my attention. The flowered tree peeps up in the midst of the sky background. This room has been a comfort and such a feeling of hope. I felt as if a part of me was being left behind. It has been such a joy and love displayed throughout my treatment.

The final treatment is complete and the tech acknowledged that everything went well with all my treatments. Before leaving the room I was presented with a certificate of completion for my treatments. This was a surprise, and I was greatly appreciative. They stated their enjoyment and pleasure in providing my treatments.

The nurse saw me before leaving expressing how great a patient I was. She gave me my discharge information and my appointment in April 2020. The administrator greeted me and mentioned that they will miss my smile. I am so grateful to all the caregivers beginning with my primary doctor, surgeon and the assistants during surgery. I am grateful for those that cared for me during my hospital stay. I am thankful for the visiting home nurses and the therapist that were instrumental in my recovery.

Celebrating the final treatment

1ST DAY OF NO MORE TREATMENTS –

September 26, 2019

What no treatment today. It was strange to awaken and realize that I would not be going to the cancer center. The wind is blowing, giving coolness in the air, with the sun shining brightly. It seemed there was something missing. Always looking forward to going to the center. Being more concerned about putting a smile on the other patient's face that didn't have one. It was as though my treatment was secondary. Not that I wasn't concerned about my healing but very concerned about keeping the other patients motivated.

2nd DAY NO MORE TREATMENTS – September 27, 2019

A new day of giving thanks and praises. Even though it's a cool and dreary day, it is still a blessing. Since I am not going to the center, this time was used to make calls to check on the sick and shut-ins. There is always someone that is in need of a kind word. Encouragement and motivation is important to keep a patient focused on staying positive while in the healing process.

Now the treatment regimen is completed and a change in the treated area begins. While receiving treatments there was no pain at all. There is a healing ointment used during the treatment and continued after treatments were done. After the first week I began to notice a change in my skin tone. The flesh began to be irritated and shedding skin. It started to become bothersome but not enough to complain. I began to remember what was told to me by the nurse at the center when issuing the healing ointment. She put emphasis on treating the area daily and often during the treatment days. Clothing touching the treated area started to become a nuisance. This is why it is so important to stay focused on the results, which is complete healing.

I realize that our energy should be spent on increasing our positive mindset that will override the negative. I am not stating that every day was great. There were days that tears were shed. The best thing of all, I did not let it hold me down. We are our worst enemy when problems show up. My family were always asking "how are you feeling", it was hard not giving them information about my bad days. Spending time in my secret closet kept me lifted up so when I was seen by anyone they would only see a smile. My husband would always want to know if I am alright, did I need anything. I love my family dearly but this was a journey that was given to me. Their concern and love was all I needed to keep me motivated.

My skin has started changing from redness back to my color tone. There has always been a lot of itching which will drive you up a wall. All this happening at the same time gave no time to think about it except finding relief. Trying to sleep became a new plan. A pillow is used to prop my left arm up to prevent it from touching the other skin area.

Anyone dealing with cancer of any kind has to control their thinking. You should not start to feel sorry for yourself. We do not know the end results but the faith we have will keep us in peace while we are on this journey. This cancer journey has made me stronger and allowed me to accept life as a greater blessing than before. There are tears of joy daily, matter of fact there are tears right now. I feel so uplifted and filled with the spirit of the Lord, fear is not in the picture.

C   CONCENTRATE ON LIFE

A   ACCEPT NO EXCUSES

N   NEVER GIVE IN

C   CENTER ON THE FUTURE

E   ENJOY THE HEALING

R   RISE UP AND LIVE

A News Article Posted on Beaumont.org

Wednesday, October 16, 2019

She was unwilling to put her health on hold because of fear

Brenda Montgomery had achieved two major milestones – retirement and having her first book published. Things were all coming together for the Detroit resident. Then, during a breast self-exam, she noticed some abnormalities in her left breast.

BREAST SELF-EXAM

"This particular night I thought would be the same as all the rest. I noticed a difference [in her breast], but kept telling myself it was nothing," Montgomery, 73, wrote in her journal.

Initially, she shrugged it off. But after the disbelief passed, Montgomery realized she should talk with her family physician, Dr. Liza Weathersby. She did not want to wait for her scheduled annual mammogram.

" ... it was not my imagination, seeking medical advice was important," wrote Montgomery. "We cannot put our health on hold because of fear."

CANCER DIAGNOSIS

Dr. Weathersby examined Montgomery. Then, she referred her to the <u>Beaumont Cancer and Breast Care Center in Farmington Hills</u> for a mammogram. The results led to more tests: an ultrasound, MRI and needle biopsies. The diagnosis – early stage breast cancer.

Montgomery admits the news was shocking. She noted in her journal, "Of course this was a big surprise and left me speechless for a moment. After yearly mammograms returning negative and many self-examinations that gave no signs of problems, this was a startling find."

TREATMENT

The medical team at the Beaumont Cancer and Breast Care Center, Farmington Hills helped Montgomery understand her treatment options. This included a breast surgeon, oncologist, radiation oncologist and nurse navigator.

In July, she had a mastectomy and, in September, she received 16 radiation treatments.

VISION BOARD

A woman of faith, Montgomery completed a 2019 vision board with other church members months before her diagnosis. Her board uses pictures, drawings and words to depict her strong religious faith, new book, love of family and hobbies.

After her diagnosis, she recalled a conversation, "Lord, I don't see cancer on my vision board." And then, she said the Lord replied, "This is one of the unforeseens."

FAMILY

Montgomery and her family had seen and coped with many unexpected events living on a sugar cane plantation in Louisiana. She was raised by grandparents who were sharecroppers. Montgomery's recently published autobiography, "Mud, Sweat and Tears," chronicles her early years.

In her book she writes, "We didn't have the best in material things, but the love we shared wouldn't be taken away."

Her grandparents taught Montgomery about family, faith, compassion, respect and hard work. She said, "They struggled, but they were overcomers."

JOURNEY

"My cancer, it's been a journey, but not one of sadness," Montgomery said, "You can't stay focused on the downs and negatives."

When she completed her radiation treatments, Montgomery experienced mixed emotions: happy her treatments were done, but sad she was no longer going to be meeting with her friends – caregivers and patients.

MOTIVATING OTHERS

Moving forward, she said, "I want to motivate others facing cancer. I'm open to sharing my story, experiences. My message – stress the importance of early cancer detection."

Instead of picking up where she left off with her autobiography, she intends to turn her recent journal into a book about her cancer journey.

Montgomery's husband, Ray, said, "Despite her cancer diagnosis and treatments, she never slowed down. She has another story to tell."

MIND, BODY AND SPIRIT

"Brenda's experience underscores the importance of periodic breast self-exams," said Dr. Weathersby. "It also helped that she has such a positive, upbeat attitude and strong support network. She's a wonderful woman and patient."

Explained Penny Widmaier, MSN, oncology nurse navigator, Beaumont Cancer and Breast Care Center, Farmington Hills, "Brenda was a delight. She was positive, with a great outlook. Her husband provided constant support. She was diligent about making it to all her appointments and was grateful for the care received from her medical team. Brenda confronted her breast cancer with mind, body and spirit."

Made in the USA
Middletown, DE
14 July 2023

35029662R00055